Button Breaker

a Treasure Troll Tale

Stephen Cosgrove

illustrated by
Diana Rice Bonin

A Golden Book • New York

Western Publishing Company, Inc., Racine, Wisconsin 53404

The Carousel ® ™
13110 NE 177th PL
Woodinville, WA 98072

Publisher: Nancy L. Cosgrove
Business Director: Terri Anderson
Creative Editor: Matt Stuart

Button Breaker

a Treasure Troll Tale by Stephen Cosgrove

Dedicated to Dave Smith, an iron man and dentist of great distinction. Though he shares the chores he still searches the mountains near San Diego for the PowerStones.

Stephen

Magic is here – for this is the land of Hodge Podge and the village of Hairst Bree. In this land and in this village live fairylike creatures called Treasure Trolls. Their laughter tinkles like crystal bells as they scamper about searching for magical little jewels called WishStones. For every troll knows that when you wish upon a WishStone all your dreams come true. When a WishStone is found, the Treasure Troll who finds it can wish upon it. All he or she needs to say is,

> "TINKLE, TWINKLE, HAIR SO FUZZY.
> TINKLE, TWINKLE, BEES GO BUZZY.
> WISH I MAY,
> WISH I MIGHT
> HAVE THE WISH I WISH TONIGHT."

And just like that the wishes are granted. Magic is here – in the very hearts of the Treasure Trolls and in the WishStones they carry.

All of the Treasure Trolls who live in the land of Hodge Podge and the village of Hairst Bree work together to do those chores that make life a little easier. They harvest the nuts and berries that grow in great abundance. They sweep their porches and houses clean of dust and golden pollen. They wash and wax; they needle and spin; they work and work until all their chores are done.

The Treasure Trolls love working together, doing all sorts of chores as their WishStones twinkle with wishes yet to be granted.

All of the Treasure Trolls love to do chores. All, that is, save for one troll who long ago thought there were boy troll chores and girl troll chores. He loved the boy troll chores, like chopping wood. He did not like the girl troll chores, like hanging the wash.

His name was Button Breaker. He wanted to be the toughest, strongest Treasure Troll that had ever lived in the land of Hodge Podge so that he would never have to do girl troll chores again. But Button Breaker was just a child, an ordinary troll of ordinary size. He wasn't too big and he wasn't too small. Day after day he did the chores that he was told to do, including chores that he thought weren't for boy trolls.

Like all Treasure Trolls, Button Breaker had a WishStone instead of a belly button. Day after day Button Breaker would stand near the Wishing Tree in the center of the village of Hairst Bree holding his WishStone firmly in his hand, wishing and wishing to be different than he was.

Every day the same thing happened – nothing at all.

Now, it was rumored in story and song that there were special stones scattered throughout the land – very special stones, indeed. These stones could grant to a Treasure Troll the gift of amazing strength. These special stones were called PowerStones. If the stories could be believed, a troll who had a PowerStone need only grasp the stone, clench his or her fist to the sky, and shout these simple words: "Ten and triple Treasure Troll. Ten and triple Treasure Troll. Tramp and trounce, jump and bounce, purple power Treasure Troll."

Then, in a flash of lightning, whoever held the PowerStone would become a PowerTroll. Muscles would ripple and the strength of three times ten trolls would be at the wish and want of but one. That troll could then lift boulders and toss them into the air like dandelion fluff.

These great stones, the PowerStones, granted great wishes. Whoever held the PowerStone could join the "Shhh!" *others* – the secret club for the owners of the PowerStones. Still, it was just a story, for nobody in the land of Hodge Podge and no one in the village of Hairst Bree ever admitted to having seen a PowerStone, let alone to having owned one.

Button Breaker wanted a PowerStone and he wanted to belong to that secret club in the worst and best of ways. Every morning, as ribbons of sunlight wrapped his room in dawn's delight, he looked at his emerald-green WishStone that had been his since birth. He looked and looked and wished and wished that his WishStone would become a PowerStone. Of all the wishes a WishStone could grant, it could never grant the wish of becoming another stone. But that never stopped Button Breaker from wishing and wanting.

Nearly every day, as he did his chores, he yearned for his wish to come true. "Oh, I wish I was a PowerTroll. I wish – oh, yes – I wish I could be a member of the 'Shhh!' *others.*"

Every day was just the same. Button Breaker did all of the chores that were asked of him before and after school. Now, doing his chores and liking his chores were two different things. Button Breaker loved chopping wood, because that was a powerful thing to do. He didn't mind mining for WishStones, for that, too, was a powerful chore to do.

He did mind washing the dishes. It didn't seem like a boy troll thing to do. And he really did mind hanging the clothes outside to dry, because that didn't seem like a powerful thing to do. He hung up his mother's nightgown and he hung up his sister's slip, pouting all the while. With squinted eyes he wished for a PowerStone that would make him too powerful to do these kinds of chores. A PowerStone that would grant him membership in the most secret of clubs – the club of the "Shhh!" *others.*

It came to pass, in the springtime when all the trolls were shearing the woolly chipmunks and spinning their wool into yarn to be woven into cloth, that Button Breaker got his wish. He had chased after a silly chipmunk, who for whatever reason didn't want to be sheared. Up and up, from foothills to mountaintops, he chased that giggling ball of fluff. Over logs and under foliage and fern they scampered, high into the craggy cliffs of Mount Wishbone. He cornered the chattering chipmunk and leaped with outstretched arms to capture the ball of fuzz. As Button Breaker jumped, the chipmunk jigged, and Button Breaker skidded to a stop into a pile of rocks.

With skinned knees and a tear in his eye, Button Breaker grabbed a rock to throw at the mischievous chipmunk. Just as he was ready to let the rock fly, Button Breaker felt a shock run down his arm. He opened his hand and looked at what he clutched. It was a round, rough purple rock that sparked with power and might.

It was a PowerStone.

Button Breaker stood with his legs shaking holding the PowerStone high above his head in his clenched fist. He gulped once and then began chanting: "Ten and triple Treasure Troll. Ten and triple Treasure Troll. Tramp and trounce, jump and bounce, purple power Treasure Troll."

The clear sky darkened with angry, rolling black clouds. The heavens grumbled and rumbled and then, in a mighty flash of lightning, Button Breaker was changed into a PowerTroll. Surprised at the sudden change, he took a hesitant step and, with his new PowerTroll strength, launched himself high into the air. He bounded about, leaping tall boulders in a single stride. He grabbed a stone in his hand and, with a simple *crunch, crunch, crinkle, crinkle,* reduced it to dust.

Button Breaker was changed. Button Breaker was now a PowerTroll. Button Breaker now could join the most secret of secret clubs – the club of the "Shhh!" *others.*

Button Breaker swaggered powerfully down the mountain to the meadows below. Animals skittered and scurried out of his way trembling in fear as this earthquake of a troll rumbled by. On his way Button Breaker pushed boulders from his path as though they were balls of fluff and not rocks at all. He kicked fallen logs into the air like jackstraws in a children's game. But this was no child.

This was Button Breaker, a Treasure Troll in possession of a PowerStone. He was on his way to take his rightful place in the most secret of secret clubs – the "Shhh!" *others.*

Down the mountain trail he walked and back to the village of Hairst Bree. There, to the amazement of all, Button Breaker exhibited his amazing strength. He lifted and bent and crushed and tossed all sorts of heavy objects as if they were feathers. All the while he looked about for the "Shhh!" *others*. But no "Shhh!" *others* came forward.

From the gabled window of their cottage, Button Breaker's mother watched, her lips turned up in a secret smile. She patiently watched and finally called, "Button Breaker! It's time to do your chores."

Button Breaker set down the seven Treasure Trolls he had hoisted upon his shoulder and, with a nod of disdain to the other trolls, he strode off to his mother and the waiting chores. Surely the "Shhh!" *others* would come when he did his chores so powerfully.

Button Breaker said not a word as he strode into the cottage where he and his family lived. He said not a word as he grabbed the ax and stepped out to the woodpile. There, with mighty blows, he chopped all the logs of Knobbily Pine into piles of kindling. Next he stacked all the rocks in the garden into a mighty stone fence surrounding the cottage. All of this he did in the blink of eye and the flex of a mighty arm.

Still, no "Shhh!" *others* stepped forward to invite him into the club. The only invitation he received was from his mother. She wanted him to do yet another chore – a chore thought by Button Breaker to be a girl troll chore. His mother asked him sweetly if he would hang the wash on the line outside.

Now Button Breaker was angry. He had not been asked to join the "Shhh!" *others.* Instead, he was being asked to hang up frilly, silky stuff. This was just too much for a PowerTroll such as he.

With muscles rippling, Button Breaker stood on his tiptoes and looked his mother in the eye. "I'll do any boy troll chore," he said in a powerful voice. "I'll chop the wood, mow the lawn and stack the rocks. I'll plow the fields, pull the stumps, pump the pump to fetch the water, and battle the beasts that threaten the herds. But mark my words, I am a PowerTroll filled with the strength of ten times triple any other troll. I only do chores that take strength. I will never do girl troll chores again. For I have the PowerStone and soon I will join the 'Shhh!' *others.*"

Button Breaker's mother smiled a gentle smile. "So, you have a PowerStone," she crooned, "and you wish to join the 'Shhh!' *others?*" She looked at her son in that special way that mothers often do. "Well, I can take you to the 'Shhh!' *others.*"

"You can?" asked Button Breaker in wide-eyed wonder. "Oh, please take me to them. Please!"

His mother nodded. But surprisingly, she didn't take Button Breaker into town or into the woods. Instead, she opened the squeaky screen and went back into the house. Mystified, Button Breaker followed.

There, in the hall, his mother stood quietly in front of a mirror. Button Breaker waited and waited and then finally said, "Well, Mother, where is the group? Where is the club? Where are the 'Shhh!' *others?*"

"Look in the mirror, my son. What do you see?"

"I see me and my mother," he snapped. "Now, where are the 'Shhh!' *others?*"

To his shock and surprise, his mother reached deep into her apron pocket and took out a stone – a special stone, a secret stone, a PowerStone. As she held it in her palm, a purple light danced down the rippling muscles of her arm.

"You. . . you," Button Breaker stuttered in surprise. "*You* are one of the 'Shhh!' *others?* But you can't be. You're a mother!"

Button Breaker's mother put her arm around his shoulder and quietly said, "Yes, my son, I am a mother. You see, there really are no girl troll chores or boy troll chores. All chores take strength and need to be done by all. As for the club you seek it was not always called the 'Shhh!' *others.* . . At first, before it was open to all, it was called the 'Mmmm!' *others* – the Mothers."

And so Button Breaker discovered, as have so many other Treasure Troll boys and girls, that there are no girl troll chores or boy troll chores. For all chores take strength and need to be done by all.

Some night, when you are supposed to be fast asleep, sneak into the kitchen where your mother is still working. Don't be surprised if you see her reach deep into her pocket and hold the PowerStone hidden there. Then listen as your mother whispers these simple words: "Ten and triple Treasure Troll. Ten and triple Treasure Troll. Tramp and trounce, jump and bounce, purple power Treasure Troll."

Just like that, you'll see her change from a mother into a PowerMomma, a "Shhh!" *other.* For to be a mother takes the strength of three times ten. All mothers have, hidden in an apron or stuffed in a pocket, a PowerStone that gives them strength to help a family grow.

Right now, all the "Shhh!" *others* are wishing on their WishStones that your wishes will come true, too.

Stephen Edward Cosgrove

...was born July 26, 1945, in Spokane, Washington.

...was raised in Boise, Idaho.

...has written and published over two hundred children's titles.

...lives now with his beloved wife Nancy, his delightful stepson Matthew, his little dog Rhubarb, Snickers the attack cat and two goldfish the size of whales in the foothills just outside Seattle, Washington.